WI
Carole

"*I love the real location*
to go and visit them al
maybe, but I can't wai

"*One day, I want to be a real kid in one of Ms. Marsh's mystery books.*
I t
I f
fi

"*F*
M
le

"*I*
m
we
Trying to figure that out is fun!"

"*Grant is cool and funny! He makes me laugh a lot!*"

"*I like that there are boys and girls of different ages in the story .*
Some mysteries I outgrow, but I can always find a favorite
character to identify with

"*They are scary, but not t*   *a lot.*
There is always food whic   *am*
there."

What Parents and Teachers Say about Carole Marsh Mysteries . . .

"I think kids love these books because they have such a wealth of detail. I know I learn a lot reading them! It's an engaging way to look at the history of any place or event. I always say I'm only going to read one chapter to the kids, but that never happens—it's always two or three, at least!"
—Librarian

"Reading the mystery and going on the field trip—Scavenger Hunt in hand—was the most fun our class ever had! It really brought the place and its history to life. They loved the real kids characters and all the humor. I loved seeing them learn that reading is an experience to enjoy!"
—4th grade teacher

"Carole Marsh is really on to something with these unique mysteries. They are so clever; kids want to read them all. The Teacher's Guides are chock full of activities, recipes, and additional fascinating information. My kids thought I was an expert on the subject—and with this tool, I felt like it!"
—3rd grade teacher

"My students loved writing their own Real Kids/Real Places mystery book! Ms. Marsh's reproducible guidelines are a real jewel. They learned about copyright and more & ended up with their own book they were so proud of!"
—Reading/Writing Teacher

"The kids seem very realistic—my children seemed to relate to the characters. Also, it is educational by expanding their knowledge about the famous places in the books."

"They are what children like: mysteries and adventures with children they can relate to."

"Encourages reading for pleasure."

"This series is great. It can be used for reluctant readers, and as a history supplement."

THE BREATHTAKING
Mystery on
Mount Everest
The Top of the World

by Carole Marsh

Band-Aid® is a registered trademark of Johnson and Johnson Consumer Companies, Inc.

Gallopade International is introducing SAT words that kids need to know in each new
book we publish. The SAT words are bold in the story. Look for this special logo
beside each word in the glossary. Happy Learning!

Gallopade is proud to be a member and supporter of these educational organizations
and associations:

American Booksellers Association
American Library Association
International Reading Association
National Association for Gifted Children
The National School Supply and Equipment Association
The National Council for the Social Studies
Museum Store Association
Association of Partners for Public Lands
Association of Booksellers for Children
Association for the Study of African American Life and History
National Alliance of Black School Educators

30 Years Ago . . .

As a mother and an author, one of the fondest periods of my life was when I decided to write mystery books for children. At this time (1979) kids were pretty much glued to the TV, something parents and teachers complained about the way they do about web surfing and blogging today.

I decided to set each mystery in a real place—a place kids could go and visit for themselves after reading the book. And I also used real children as characters. Usually a couple of my own children served as characters, and I had no trouble recruiting kids from the book's location to also be characters.

Also, I wanted all the kids—boys and girls of all ages—to participate in solving the mystery. And, I wanted kids to learn something as they read. Something about the history of the location. And I wanted the stories to be funny. That formula of real+scary+smart+fun served me well.

I love getting letters from teachers and parents who say they read the book with their class or child, then visited the historic site and saw all the places in the mystery for themselves. What's so great about that? What's great is that you and your children have an experience that bonds you together forever. Something you shared. Something you both cared about at the time. Something that crossed all age levels—a good story, a good scare, a good laugh!

30 years later,

Carole Marsh

Hey, kids! As you see—here we are ready to embark on another of our exciting Carole Marsh Mystery adventures! You know, in "real life," I keep very close tabs on Christina, Grant, and their friends when we travel. However, in the mystery books, they always seem to slip away from Papa and me so that they can try to solve the mystery on their own!

I hope you will go to www.carolemarshmysteries.com and apply to be a character in a future mystery book! Well, the *Mystery Girl* is all tuned up and ready for "take-off!"

Gotta go... Papa says so! Wonder what I've forgotten this time?

Happy "Armchair Travel" Reading,

Mimi

About the Characters

 **Christina**, age 10: Mysterious things really do happen to her! Hobbies: soccer, Girl Scouts, anything crafty, hanging out with Mimi, and going on new adventures.

 Grant, age 7: Always manages to fall off boats, back into cactuses, and find strange clues—even in real life! Hobbies: camping, baseball, computer games, math, and hanging out with Papa.

 **Mimi** is Carole Marsh, children's book author and creator of Carole Marsh Mysteries, Around the World in 80 Mysteries, Three Amigos Mysteries, Baby's First Mysteries, and many others.

 **Papa** is Bob Longmeyer, the author's real-life husband, who really does wear a tuxedo, cowboy boots and hat, fly an airplane, captain a boat, speak in a booming voice, and laugh a lot!

Travel around the world with Christina and Grant as they visit famous places in 80 countries, and experience the mysterious happenings that always seem to follow them!

Books in This Series

Table of Contents

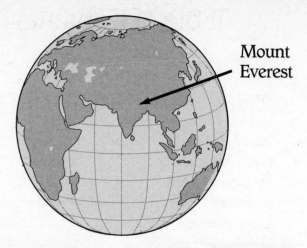

Mount Everest

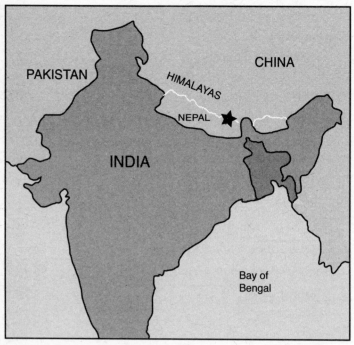

PAKISTAN

CHINA

HIMALAYAS

NEPAL

INDIA

Bay of
Bengal

SCURRYING SKIVVIES

SCREEEEECH!

Christina woke up with a start. Tires squealed with urgency in front of her grandparents' house. She threw back her covers and dashed to the window. Flinging back the curtains, all she could see was the flash of a silver bumper disappearing in a black cloud of exhaust fumes and burning rubber. The family dog, Clue, barked ferociously.

She watched Mimi, Papa, and Uncle Mike scurry across the yard to look at the still-smoking tire marks on the pavement. Christina rushed out to join them. Her bare feet left dark footprints in the dew-soaked grass.

"What's going on?" Christina asked.

"Don't know," Papa answered in a deep, raspy voice that told her he hadn't had his first cup of coffee. "Guess somebody was in a big hurry, or at least Clue helped them get in a big hurry."

"That a boy, Clue," Christina said, patting the bloodhound's head. "Think it could've been that teenager down the street?"

Mimi laughed. "Not at this time of the morning!" she said. "Most teenagers don't get up before noon on Saturday!"

"Oh, yeah!" exclaimed Christina excitedly. "For a second I forgot that it's Saturday—the day we're leaving for the biggest adventure of our lives!"

"You said it!" Uncle Mike agreed. "This is the day I've been dreaming of for the past two years!"

Christina could see his van in the driveway stuffed with bags and bags of gear and equipment. She shivered with excitement. Christina had traveled all over the United States and much of the world with her little brother Grant, grandfather Papa, and grandmother Mimi, better known to many as mystery writer Carole Marsh. Every place they went was always fascinating with lots of interesting things to see and learn, but this trip was different. This was not a typical place tourists would choose. Most wouldn't have the courage to go to a place so cold, isolated, and deadly!

Ten-year-old Christina smiled proudly at her tall, handsome uncle, Mimi's only son. He and his friend Dave had lifted weights, climbed more rock walls than a gecko, and run for miles and miles to prepare. Now they were ready to climb the tallest mountain in the world—Mount Everest!

"HOW EMBARRASSING!" someone yelled from the front porch. They all turned at once and saw that it was Grant.

"Why are you all standing out here in your skivvies?" he asked.

Christina, Papa, and Mimi exchanged looks and burst into laughter. They suddenly realized that in the excitement of the moment, they had rushed out without even grabbing a robe. Only Uncle Mike, who had just arrived when the commotion took place, was fully dressed. Papa had pulled on his cowboy boots. But the only other thing he was wearing was his sleeping shorts covered in red airplanes that looked a lot like his own little red and white plane, *Mystery Girl.*

Mimi's short blond hair had not seen a comb yet and looked like a bird's nest on top of her head. She was wearing a long beige gown with red sequined hearts around the neck.

Christina shivered again, this time from the cool breeze. Her favorite jammies, covered with running horses, were not made for romping outside on a chilly, spring morning.

"Brrrrr," Christina said through chattering teeth. "I sure could use a cup of your hot chocolate, Mimi!"

Grant waved frantically for them to come inside. Christina skittered across the grass, trying to step back into the footprints she had made on the way out. On her right, she could see the jumble of footprints made by Uncle Mike, Mimi, Papa, and Clue. But on her left, Christina noticed other marks on the grass that were not shaped like feet at all. A curious line of triangles pointed toward the line of shrubs in front of the porch. Christina let her eyes follow the trail until she saw it. Something was sparkling in one of the shrubs!

iCY OMEN

Christina was no stranger to mystery. During every trip with her grandparents, a tangled web of mystery often caught her and Grant the way a spider catches buzzing flies. She wouldn't be surprised to find a mystery waiting for them at Mount Everest, but she was surprised by a mystery beginning before they even left their home in Peachtree City, Georgia!

"Pssst!" Christina called to Grant as he was about to follow the adults inside.

She reached into the shrubs and pulled out a black envelope with gold metallic writing on it, and jumped up on the porch.

"What's that?" Grant asked, peering at the strange note.

"Whoever took off in such a hurry this morning must have delivered it," answered

Christina. She traced her fingers over writing that looked like none she had ever seen. "I don't see how the note could be meant for any of us," she said. "It's not written in English!"

Christina ran her finger under the flap and opened the envelope like something inside might bite her. Gingerly she pulled out a note on thick black paper. Several slivers of ice fell out and shattered on the porch floor in a spray of sparkling crystals. Squiggly writing in the same gold ink looked like it was hanging upside down from the lines that stretched across the page. It was beautiful, but mysterious. At the bottom was a drawing of a pair of eyes and a nose that looked like a question mark.

"Who sends a letter on black paper in a black envelope with ice inside?" Grant asked. "Seems sort of creepy. Don't you think you should show it to the adults?"

"No, Grant," Christina answered. "Uncle Mike and Dave have enough worries about their climb—like staying alive! I don't want to give them anything else to worry about."

In the kitchen, Mimi watched colorful cups of hot chocolate spin in the microwave like a carousel. Papa sipped his coffee and asked, "Are you kids ready to fly to the other side of the world?"

"All packed!" Christina said proudly.

"And I have plenty of games," Grant quickly added.

Mimi plunked their hot chocolate down in front of them. "You understand this is probably the longest flight you've ever taken," she said.

"How long will it take us to get there and land on Mount Everest?" Grant asked.

Christina rolled her eyes. "Oh, Grant," she said. "You don't land on Mount Everest!"

"Yeah," Uncle Mike said. "If you could simply fly a plane to the top and land, what would be the purpose of us climbing it?"

"Right," said Grant, nodding. "Then where do we land?"

Papa pulled a small globe from a shelf and spun it around. He stopped it with his thick finger. "This is India," he said, "and this is

China. We are flying into Nepal, this little sliver of country in between."

"Wow!" Grant said. "It doesn't look big enough to land a plane in!"

Papa laughed loudly. "It's larger than it looks on the globe," he said. "I promise! It's about the same size as Florida. You kids are lucky to get to visit Nepal. When I was a kid, the country was closed to visitors. It wasn't opened until 1951. Two years later something very exciting happened."

"I know!" Christina cried. "In 1953, Sir Edmund Hillary reached the summit of Mount Everest!"

Uncle Mike's friend Dave bounded into the kitchen wearing an excited grin. "Everybody got your crampons packed?" he asked.

"I don't think so," Grant said, concerned. "What are crampons?"

"They're spikes that you strap to your boots so you can climb on ice and packed snow," Dave answered.

Mimi laughed. "My high heels can do that!"

Icy Omen

Christina chuckled at Mimi, but couldn't help but worry about the ominous black note. *What did it mean? Was it a warning?*

PROMISES, PROMISES

"Avalanche!" Christina yelled. She ran as fast as she could, but the thundering wall of snow was gaining on her. The shelter of a big rock lay ahead. *Can I make it before the snow swallows me?* she wondered, panicked. Suddenly, Christina felt a strong hand grab her shoulder. *Was it pulling her to safety?*

"Hey!" Uncle Mike said, shaking Christina. "Wake up, crew chief! We're about to land in Kathmandu, capital city of Nepal!"

Christina swallowed hard and licked her dry lips, thankful that she had only been dreaming. Since Uncle Mike had named her crew chief and Grant assistant crew chief for the expedition, safety concerns were creeping into her dreams.

Grant, curled up in the seat beside her, stretched his arms and legs. "It's about time," he said. "It'll probably take me a long time to get my land legs again!"

"You're right," Uncle Mike agreed. "The jet lag after a flight this long is a killer. That's why we're going to rest for a day in Kathmandu before the next leg of our adventure to the Himalayas."

"Wait a minute," Grant said. "I thought we were going to Mount Everest!"

Uncle Mike tousled Grant's curly blonde hair. "Everest is in the Himalayan Mountains, silly!"

Papa yawned loudly. "This adventure's got more legs than a five-legged cow!" he said.

Mimi patted Papa's arm. "Yes," she agreed, "but it's going to help me write the best mystery I've ever written!"

Christina loved all of Mimi's mysteries, but this one would be special. Uncle Mike and Dave, who both helped Mimi with her books, would be able to tell her exactly what they saw and felt as they climbed Everest—if they made it!

Tribhuvan International Airport was sleek and modern, but an ancient vehicle—a rickshaw—was taking them through Kathmandu to their hotel.

"*Namaste!*" a young man said, with a brilliant white smile. He had ebony hair and smooth skin the color of milk chocolate. Christina and Grant crawled into the covered, two-wheeled cart hooked to his bicycle. Christina, who didn't understand his language, Nepali, smiled back. She would later learn that *namaste* was a lot like *aloha* in Hawaii. It means both hello and goodbye.

Christina poked her hand through the little window in the back of the rickshaw and waved at Mimi and Papa behind them. Uncle Mike and Dave had taken a regular taxi so they could haul all their gear.

"We need one of these so you can pull me around!" Christina whispered to Grant, who was busy checking the compass Uncle Mike had given him.

"Yeah—right!" Grant replied, frowning.

Kathmandu was unlike any city Christina had seen. Papa had said Nepal was one of the poorest countries in the world, but Christina couldn't believe how fancy some of the buildings were. Around windows were carved wood that looked like lace. Tall shrines, many with three-sectioned, pagoda-style roofs, pointed to the sky. In the busy markets, merchants sold everything from scary masks to smelly fish.

An old man with a wild gray beard sat on a leopard skin and held out a bowl for donations. Temple bells clanged and the air was filled with exotic music from the *sarangi*, the most popular instrument in Nepal. Its four strings, played with a bow like a violin, sounded like a fiddle had married a set of bagpipes.

Mimi and Papa's rickshaw sped around them and then stopped suddenly. Mimi hopped out.

"I want to get a picture of this!" she yelled. She aimed her camera at a colorful, but terrifying statue. It had six arms, a toothy, growling scowl, coiled golden serpents for earrings and bracelets, and a crown with skulls on it.

"This is Kalbhairav," Mimi explained. "People come here to make promises they plan to keep."

"Looks like a nightmare!" Christina exclaimed.

"Well, here's my promise," Grant said. "Uncle Mike and Dave will make it to the top of Mount Everest!"

"I certainly hope so, Grant," Mimi replied, staring at the majestic Himalayas in the distance. "The legend says that if someone breaks that promise, they will spit blood!"

4

MONKEY BUSINESS

"Look at the eyes!" Christina exclaimed. "Those are the same eyes on the black letter!"

The staring eyes, painted on all four sides of a shrine that looked like a hill wearing a fancy gold hat, captured Mimi's interest too.

"It's spectacular!" she exclaimed, snapping pictures. "This shrine is called Swayambhunath. It is considered sacred to both the Hindus and Buddhists. Its nickname is the 'monkey temple' because a lot of wild monkeys live here."

"Sway what?" Grant asked. "I think I like 'monkey temple' better!"

A red and gold Buddha statue sat peacefully at the bottom of a long stairway leading to the shrine. Several small, brown rhesus monkeys played on top of his head. One of them bared his teeth and fussed at Grant. Grant grinned and hopped around, scratching under his arms.

OOH OOH!

AHH AHH!

OOH OOH!

AHH AHH!

"Monkey see, monkey do!" Christina said with a snicker.

"Monkeys are considered sacred," Mimi said. "You shouldn't make fun of them, Grant."

"Why are there so many shrines and statues in Nepal?" Christina asked.

"The people are from different cultures and have different religions," Mimi explained. "It's mainly a Hindu kingdom, but there are also many Buddhists."

"To bad there's not a statue to make wishes on," Grant said. "I'd wish for a big, juicy hamburger! I'm starving!"

Mimi quickly clamped her hand over Grant's mouth. "Pleeease don't say anything about eating beef while we're here," she begged. "The cow is also considered a sacred animal in Nepal. Hindus don't eat them."

As Grant tried to imagine a life without hamburgers, one of the monkeys scampered off the statue and onto the rickshaw.

"Hey!" Grant yelled. "Get away from there!"

It was too late. The monkey reached into his unzipped backpack and grabbed the compass. In its place he left a chunk of melting ice and a small stone with more strange writing.

"Oh no!" Grant whined. "I needed that compass for our expedition!"

Christina looked up at the eyes on the shrine. She felt like they were watching her. *Had the person who left the note in Mimi's shrubs followed them here? And what was written on that stone?*

TOO MANY LEGS!

Christina gripped the arms of her seat like her life depended on it. Maybe it did! She gazed out the window of the small, twin-engine plane Papa had called a puddle jumper, carrying them from Kathmandu to Lukla, Nepal—the second leg of their adventure. Below, mountains that had looked small from Kathmandu loomed beneath them. White clouds covered their tops like flowing scarves, and the green of early spring climbed them like brave mountaineers.

When the plane started its descent, Christina couldn't believe her eyes. "You've got to be kidding!" she cried.

They were aimed for a thin ribbon of runway that dropped right off the edge of a cliff!

"Don't worry," Papa assured her. "They land planes here every day."

"Yes," she answered eyeing the wreckage of a plane below, "but how many of those are crash landings?"

Christina squeezed her eyes shut as the plane started to vibrate. If they missed the runway and smashed into the side of a mountain, she didn't want to watch.

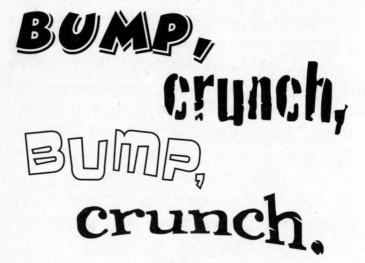

BUMP, crunch, BUMP, crunch.

The plane's tires hit the gravel and their expedition equipment bounced and clattered.

Christina breathed a sigh of relief, but felt strange. Outside, the air was cooler and thinner than Kathmandu. She wobbled off the plane.

"Whoa, there!" Dave said, steadying her. "Are you feeling all right?"

"Just a little dizzy and my head hurts a little," she answered.

"Probably a touch of altitude sickness," he said. "Why don't you get an aspirin from Mimi and something to drink inside the airport? Just remember not to drink the water. That's never a good idea in a foreign country because your body's not used to all the local germies!"

Grant, however, was energetic as a temple monkey. "The hills are aliiiiive, with the sound of muuuuusic!" he sang, whirling with his arms outstretched.

"You've been watching too many old movies with Mimi," Christina said. "Besides, *The Sound of Music* took place in the Austrian Alps, not the Himalayan Mountains."

"Stick some Band-Aids in your pockets, so you'll be ready for blisters!" Uncle Mike warned as he unloaded the last piece of gear from the plane.

Christina sipped her soda. The aspirin was working already. "What do you mean, Uncle Mike?" she asked. "I've got on my hiking boots and thick socks."

"It's a tough hike to our next stop, Namche Bazaar," he said.

"I'm ready!" Mimi exclaimed, modeling her red hiking boots, probably a rare sight in the Himalayas.

"Me too!" Papa said holding the hiking stick he had carved himself. "But I'm sorta worried about carryin' all this gear!"

"Wait right here!" Uncle Mike commanded. He galloped behind a nearby shed.

Too Many Legs!

In a moment, Christina heard a commotion. In the shed's shadow suddenly appeared a frightening shaggy head with horns! *Had a mountain monster mangled her uncle?*

6

YAKETY YAK

Uncle Mike stumbled from the shed, brushing off his pants and running his fingers through his messy hair. He tugged on a red, blue, and gold braided rope. Finally, he pulled a strange creature into the light. It had curving horns like a cow, long, shaggy fur like a llama, and a furry tail. A bell around its neck clanked with every step.

"Guess I startled him at first," Uncle Mike said, wiping his brow. He gave the beast a pat on the neck. "But we're friends now, aren't we, fella?"

"What is that?!" Grant yelled.

Mimi answered. "If I'm not mistaken, that is a yak."

"What does a yak do?" Grant asked.

"Well, he doesn't talk back," Papa said with a hearty laugh.

Mimi rolled her eyes at Papa's reference to a song from their day—"Yakety Yak, Don't Talk Back!" Mimi had played it once or twice for Christina when she was little.

"Since I doubt we could carry all this gear on our backs, our furry friend is gonna be our station wagon," Uncle Mike said.

Christina stroked the beast's long, coarse fur. He was mostly black with a band of white across his shoulders and halfway up each of his legs. "What's his name?" she asked.

"I have no idea," Uncle Mike answered. "But he probably doesn't understand English anyway."

"He looks like he's wearing socks," Grant observed while patting the yak's head. "Let's call him Socks!"

About that time, the furry creature let out a loud snorting sneeze. Grant received the full blast. "Yuk!" he cried. "Yak boogies!"

After a long day on the rocky, winding trail with only occasional stops to ooh and aah over a beautiful mountain scene or wash the dust from their throats with a drink of water, Christina wished Socks could carry her. She was lagging behind everyone else when she heard something behind her. A large rock plummeted from a **crag** above.

Christina jumped just in time to miss the bone-crushing boulder. It hit the trail with a heavy thud, bounced, and skipped down the mountainside.

"That was close," Papa said, giving Christina a hug when the dust had settled. "I'll be glad when we have our *sherpa* along."

Christina's heart pounded in her chest, like someone wanting out of a locked door. *Was the falling rock an accident or did someone push it?* she fretted.

"What do these sherpas look like?" Grant asked Uncle Mike once they started walking again. "Are they shaggy like yaks?"

"First of all," Uncle Mike began, "sherpas are not animals, they are people. Their ancestors crossed the Himalayas from Tibet, a Chinese province east of Nepal. In fact, sherpa means "person from the east." They are famous for their mountaineering skills and I've hired one to be our guide. Every one has heard of Sir Edmund Hillary, but chances are he couldn't have made it without his sherpa guide, Tenzing Norgay."

Christina suddenly stopped dead in her tracks. She could see a village on the side of a mountain. The red and blue-roofed buildings looked like they were hanging on for dear life!

"Please tell me that's Namche Bazaar," she said hopefully.

"Yeah!" Grant said. "I'm so hungry I could eat a yak. Sorry, Socks!"

The sun was slinking behind a line of snow-crested mountains as they stumbled down the steep trail to the village. Two stones with carved writing similar to the black letter stood near the entrance. They were as tall as Papa! Christina ran her fingers over them like a blind person reading Braille.

Christina tripped over a pair of legs and landed face first in the dust.

"So sorry!" a startled man told her as she rose to her feet. "*Namaste.* Welcome to Namche Bazaar."

"You speak English!" Christina cried in surprise through labored breaths.

"Yes, of course!" he said. "Most of the younger sherpas do."

"Pemba?" Uncle Mike asked.

"Yes!" the man answered. "*Namaste!* You are Mike?"

"Yes," Uncle Mike answered.

"Are you ready to face the mighty Sagarmatha?" he said pointing.

Grant was confused. "Is that the town bully?" he asked.

"No," Mimi said as she stared in awe at the horizon. "That's the Nepali name for Mount Everest. It's the one that's shaped like a snow-covered, three-sided pyramid."

Christina shaded her eyes with her hands and caught her first sight of the majestic mountain towering over those around it. It was still far away, but absolutely massive.

She felt a tingle claw its way up her spine like a frightened cat. *Was she ready to face the mountain? Was there someone who wanted to make sure she wasn't?*

IT'S ALTITUDE, DUDE

Pemba noticed that Christina was struggling to catch her breath. "You have elevation sickness," he said. "That's why you must rest for a day at this **altitude** to let your body get used to the height."

"Why is Christina having problems with alti-DUDE when she's a girl?" Grant asked.

Mimi laughed a tired laugh. "It's alti-TUDE," she pronounced. "When people move from a low elevation that is close to sea level, like our home in Georgia, to a high elevation like this, it's hard for our bodies to take in enough air. Because the higher you go, the thinner the air is."

"That's why we will have to wear oxygen when we climb Everest," Uncle Mike explained.

"Why doesn't he get ALTI-TUDE sickness?" Grant asked, pointing at Pemba and trying his best to say it correctly.

Pemba answered, "I was born here. My people breathe much faster than lowlanders to be able to take in the oxygen we need. You will all feel better when you get acclimated," he said.

"Does it hurt to get acclimated?" Grant asked. "It's not a shot, is it?"

"Noooo, Grant," Papa said, leaning on his walking stick. "That just means to get used to something."

Before they continued into the village, Christina had to know about the curious stones.

"They are called *Mani* stones," Pemba explained. "They have prayers written on them."

Namche Bazaar was an unusual place where shaggy yaks with their gently tinkling bells roamed the village like honored residents. At the same time, the village had electric lights and even a sign offering internet service! Shops offered all kinds of goods and restaurants offered all kinds of food—even pizza. Best of all was the warm, comforting aroma of fresh-baked rolls wafting from a bakery.

Pemba's cozy home was also a place of contrasts. On the way inside, he pulled two discs that looked like mud from the side of his house. Once inside, he placed them in the fireplace.

"What's he doing?" Grant whispered to Dave.

"Adding dung to the fire," Dave answered.

"What's that?" Grant asked.

"Dried yak poop," said Dave. "Sherpas burn it instead of firewood."

"Ewww!" Grant exclaimed.

No matter what, Christina was happy to feel the warmth from the fire. But she was shocked to see two children watching a cartoon on television. Pemba saw the look on their faces. "These are my children, Lhakpa Sherpa and Dawa Sherpa."

Grant and Christina exchanged amazed looks when he called them sherpa. "You mean they're guides already?"

"Many Westerners make that mistake," Pemba explained. "You see, all my people have the same last name, Sherpa. Our first names are given depending on which day of the week we are born. Pemba is for Saturday, Dawa is for Monday and Lhakpa is for Wednesday. The children smiled at Christina and Grant and waved for them to join them at the television. It was nice to see people their own age!

"*Namaste,*" they said at the same time. "You are surprised we have television?" Dawa asked. She spoke English as well as her father.

"Yes," Christina answered. "Namche is so far away from everything and there aren't even any roads!"

"Our father said we have many things he didn't have when he was a boy because the tourists like you have provided a way for sherpas to make a living," Dawa explained. "He said if there were no tourists, we'd have to grow potatoes to survive like his father and grandfather did. We also have Sir Edmund

Hillary to thank for much progress. He even built a school for our people."

"But there are some people who think the tourists are bad for the mountains," Lhakpa added. "They say they are destroying the Sherpa traditions."

"The worst thing about the tourists," Dawa said, "is the trash they leave behind on the mountain. Some people call Everest the world's highest garbage dump."

"That's a shame," said Christina. "It's such a beautiful place. Why do people leave their litter there?"

"Most people are just worried about surviving and making it home," Dawa said. "Since everything has to be carried, it's easier to leave the old oxygen bottles and other trash right there on the mountain."

Pemba's wife smiled sweetly from the kitchen where she was pouring steaming liquid into small bowls. She brought them to Christina and Grant.

"Our mother doesn't speak much English," Lhakpa said.

"And she still wears the traditional angee dress of our people," Dawa said, seeming embarrassed about her mother's old-fashioned ways.

Christina smiled and nodded her thanks. "What is this?" she asked.

"Sherpa tea," Dawa answered.

"I love hot tea!" Christina declared drawing in a long slurp. But her face showed them this was unlike any tea she'd had before.

Christina smiled politely as she sat her tea aside. Grant was not so subtle. "Yuk," he said. "What's in this?"

"Salt and yak butter," Lhakpa said, laughing at his guest.

While the adults made plans for the expedition, Christina thought about the mystery that had tortured her since they left Georgia.

"Is English the only language you speak?" she asked Pemba's kids.

"We also speak Nepali," said Dawa.

Christina was unsure what kind of language was on the black letter, but decided to take a chance. She pulled it from her pocket and showed them.

Dawa and Lhakpa huddled over it. "This is Nepali!" Dawa said with a big smile. But as she read, her smile turned to a frown. When she reached the bottom of the letter, she gasped and gave Lhakpa a worried look. "This is not good," she said. "This is not good at all..."

STAY AWAY!

Before Dawa could explain the letter's contents, Uncle Mike told them it was time to go. Pemba led them up a long and steep hill to a hotel famous as the highest in the world—the Everest View Hotel.

"You all must rest!" Pemba ordered when he told them goodbye. "I will take good care of your yak!"

The oxygen pumped into the room she shared with Grant made Christina feel better almost immediately. The hotel was luxurious, especially after a hard day of walking. Christina rubbed her aching feet and flopped back on the soft bed...

"Tia! Tia!" Grant said, shaking her bed. Christina hadn't even realized that she had fallen asleep and already the early morning light was peeping through the curtains.

"It's time for breakfast!" Grant said. "Everyone's waiting for us!"

"You go ahead, Grant," Christina said. "I want to wash up first."

When Grant was gone, Christina opened the curtains and gasped at the breathtaking view of Mount Everest. It looked like a giant, icy pyramid. But was this mighty mountain inviting them to come and explore, or trying to scare them away?

Dawa and Lhapka had come with their father who was still discussing expedition plans with Uncle Mike and Dave. Everyone was trying the traditional sherpa breakfast of *tsampa* on the patio. The morning air was cool and crisp, but the *tsampa*, which looked sort of like oatmeal, was warm and filling. Christina liked it better than the yak tea. Eagerly, she pulled the black letter out of her pocket and gave it to Dawa.

"Please explain what it means," she begged.

"The letter is warning you to stay away from Chomolungma," she said.

"What does that have to do with Mount Everest?" Grant asked.

"Chomolungma is the sherpa name for Everest," she explained.

"Well, why is it called Everest too?" asked Grant.

"The mountain was named Everest after a British surveyor, Sir George Everest. While mapping India, he found that it was the highest mountain in the world," Dawa said.

"So, there are three names for the mountain," Christina said. "Everest, Sagarmatha, and Chomolungma."

"That's right," said Dawa. "But who is it that wants you to stay away? Do you have an enemy?"

"Not that I know of," Christina answered.

Suddenly, Christina remembered the small, carved stone the temple monkey had left in place of Grant's compass. Clank! She slapped it down on the table. "Now, Dawa, look at this and tell me what the writing says," Christina asked.

Dawa's brows knitted in concentration. "This is in an ancient script I don't understand," she said.

Lhakpa had been quiet until now. "Maybe the monks would know," he said.

"Very good," Dawa agreed. "We will stop for a rest at Tengboche Monastery on the way to Base Camp!"

"What do you mean?" Christina asked.

"Lhakpa and I are going with you!" Dawa replied with a big grin. "This will be our third trip to Base Camp!"

Christina was relieved to have Sherpa children joining them. Uncle Mike had named her crew chief, but she really didn't know much about mountain climbing. Plus, she still had a touch of altitude sickness.

Mimi finished her breakfast and looked over at the children. "Today is your last chance," she remarked, "to buy anything before we hit the trail again tomorrow. Why don't you go shopping for trail snacks?"

"You don't have to say that twice!" Grant said. "I'll get something for Socks too!" He shot

Mimi a mischievous grin. "What's a good snack for a yak?"

Mimi caught on quick. "I'd say 'hay in a pack or a sack would be a good snack for a yak,'" she rhymed.

The children laughed and thanked Mimi for the silver coins she placed in their hands.

On the way to the market, Christina noticed a woman in high heels. It was an odd sight in a place where almost everyone wore sneakers or hiking boots. Even more odd was the footprint she noticed in the dust. It was a triangle like the one in Mimi's yard! *Could this be the person who delivered the note?* Christina quickly turned to see if she could get a good look at the woman, but she was gone.

It didn't take Grant long to find plenty of snacks at a Namche market. He emptied a basketful on the counter.

"That will be five *rupee*," the store clerk told him.

Grant looked at Christina in horror. "She wants rubies," he whispered. "All I have are these coins!"

"RuPEES are what the money here is called," Lhakpa explained and helped Grant count out the coins he needed.

On their way out, Christina noticed a man dressed in a chuba, a long colorful robe made of yak wool. The bright green ski cap on his head looked out of place. He was whispering to someone standing in the shadow of colorful parkas hanging beside ice picks and other mountain climbing equipment. Christina couldn't help hearing a woman's voice say, "We'll be first. We have to be first!"

When the children passed, the man in the green cap glared at them and growled, "Children have no business in the abode of the gods."

A LAMA DOESN'T SPIT

"WHOA!" Uncle Mike begged Socks. "Easy, fella!" He was trying to place the last pack on the shaggy beast's back, but he wanted none of it. He stamped his feet and snorted, moving nervously from side to side.

"I told you not to bring so much luggage," Papa teased Mimi. "You're about to break our poor yak's back."

Everyone chuckled except Pemba, who was watching the animal's mood carefully. "He senses something that frightens him," he said, scanning the skyline. "It could be a wild animal or even the weather. We should keep our eyes open!"

It was not a reassuring way to start a long trek in rugged terrain where little help would be available if something went wrong. But wild animals and weather were the least of Christina's worries. She was concerned about the letter's ominous warning, the mysterious writing on the stone, and now, the gruff warning in the market. Christina adjusted the pack on her back. "What did he mean about the abode of the gods?" she asked Dawa.

"In Sherpa legend," Dawa answered, "Mount Everest and the mountains around it are where the gods lived. Because of this people are not supposed to walk on them."

"Now you tell me!" Christina said.

"Don't worry," said Dawa. "It's only a legend."

"Help me!" Grant hollered. "Somebody help!" He was lying on his back, flailing his arms and legs like an upside-down turtle.

Lhakpa pulled him to his feet and helped him brush the dust off his pack and pants. "It looks like your Mimi is not the only one who packed too much!" he laughed. "Maybe you should take some things out!"

The kids helped Grant pull the heavy pack off his back. When he unzipped it, he found several big rocks inside.

Dave roared with laughter. "Looks like you fell for the oldest hiker gag in the book," he said, giving Lhakpa a high-five for helping him with the prank.

"Very funny!" said Grant. Then he giggled. "I'll have to remember that trick!"

Tall green fir trees leaned over the trail, peeking at the valley below. The enchanted scene reminded Christina of a storybook. She even wondered if someone might leave a trail of bread crumbs for them to follow. After several hours on the forested trail, delicate pink flowers covering a hillside greeted them. Mimi said they were rhododendrons. They reminded Christina of the azaleas in her yard at home.

"Just ahead is Tengboche Monastery," Lhakpa promised.

Vicious dragon statues of red, green, and gold guarded the gate with snarling teeth. Inside, the temple was a peaceful, soothing place. Monks wearing long maroon robes shuffled into a large stone building. The adults sat down on a low rock wall and

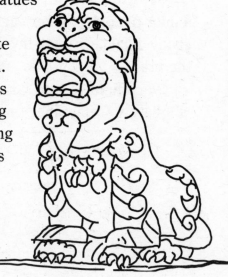

started pulling water from their packs. The kids had other ideas.

"We should follow them inside," Dawa whispered. "Maybe we could see the *lama*."

"They have a llama in there?" Grant asked. "One of them spit on me at the zoo once!"

"No," Dawa said. "I think you are confused. The lama is the spiritual leader of this monastery."

The kids quietly fell in line behind the monks who were already murmuring some sort of chant. They tiptoed down a dark hallway into a dimly lighted, but brightly painted room. The walls and even the ceiling were covered with paintings, many of them of Buddha. There was also a statue of Buddha that seemed to watch their every move. It was unlike any church Christina had ever seen!

At the front, an older monk led chants Christina and Grant could not understand. After a while, the monks slowly rose to leave, but the lama, who sat on a colorful cushion, motioned for the kids to come to him. It was almost like the

Wizard of Oz motioning Dorothy and her friends to come forward.

"Hey!" Grant whispered. "He sits criss-cross applesauce just like we do at school!"

The lama placed a white *khata*, or scarf, around each of their necks. "You are going to Chomolungma?" he asked.

"Yes," Christina answered, proud that she had learned the mountain's local name.

"I will bless your journey," the lama said.

When he was finished, Christina remembered the stone that the monkey had left in Grant's backpack. She pulled it out of her pocket. "Could you please tell us what this means?" she asked.

The lama turned the stone in his hands, reading the ancient words. He looked at them with great concern in his eyes...

10

ABOMINABLE SNOWMAN

"Are you children traveling alone?" the lama asked.

After they assured him they were not, he told them, "This is an ancient warning. It says the *yeti* will guard the abode of the gods."

With that, the lama rose. "Beware and watch for the warnings," he said and quietly left the room. Christina and Grant were filled with questions. But Dawa and Lhakpa had fearful looks on their faces.

"I'm not sure we should go to Everest," Dawa said.

"That is a scary warning," Lhakpa agreed.

"What's it all about?" Christina asked. "And what's a yeti?"

Dawa shuddered. "I do not want to say its name," she said. "It is a powerful and terrible creature that lives in the Himalayas. Many people do not believe that it is real. But when my mother was young, a girl from her village saw one kill three yaks by breaking their necks!"

"Yes," said Lhakpa. "Many people have heard them howling at night."

When they stopped for the night at a tiny stone lodge, everyone hungrily slurped bowls of thick potato soup called *shakpa*. Christina asked Uncle Mike and Dave, "Have you ever heard of the yeti?"

"Shhh!" Dave said. "Sherpas don't like to talk about him."

"We know!" Christina complained. "That's why I want you to tell us about him."

"According to legend," Uncle Mike said, "the yeti is a large shaggy creature, much stronger than any human being. Did you know that Sir Edmund Hillary and Tenzing Norgay photographed a giant footprint in the snow that could have belonged to a yeti?"

Christina and Grant's eyes grew large. "Wow!" Grant said. "So they really are real!"

"No one has ever proven for sure the yeti exists," Uncle Mike explained. "Some people believe the footprints just belong to large bears that live in the Himalayas."

"That sounds a lot like the legend of Bigfoot," Christina said. "But I wonder why we've never heard of a yeti."

"Maybe you have," Dave said. "He has another name as well—the **Abominable Snowman!**"

A BRIDGE AND A PRAYER

"Brrr!" Christina shivered from the piercing cold. After five days of hiking she was excited that they were to finally reach Base Camp today!

"Better get used to that feeling," Dave warned.

"I'm prepared!" Grant said, zipping his puffy, fur-lined parka. "I feel like an inside-out-yeti!"

Namche had been more than 11,000 feet above sea level and Base Camp would be at 17,500 feet. The top of Everest was actually five miles above sea level!

In their thick, hooded parkas, for the first time they all looked like explorers in a foreign environment. Christina could only imagine how much courage it had taken for Hillary and Norgay to make the journey—especially after seeing those giant footprints. And they didn't even have satellite phones and GPS like most modern climbers!

Ice clung to the mountainsides and patches of snow crunched under their feet like they were walking on snow cones. The wind whistled louder than the occasional bird they saw.

Christina was surprised when the trail started down a steep slope. She could hear the steady rush of water. They had crossed many aqua blue mountain streams, but this one sounded much larger. The sound grew louder and louder until Grant finally spotted something that made him yell, "How cool is that!"

To Christina it didn't look cool. It was terrifying!

Swinging between two rocky cliffs was a narrow suspension bridge. Ropes on either side held up thin wooden planks that danced in the icy breeze. Below it an icy mountain river churned violently.

The rocky trails that skirted mountain edges were scary, but doable. This was something else. Socks seemed to feel the same way. He sniffed the air and shook his shaggy head.

Along the entire length of the bridge, colorful flags printed with faded words flapped in the wind. Christina had noticed these flags several places during their journey and finally asked Dawa, "What are these flags for?"

"Those are prayer flags," she answered. "They are asking for blessings, safety, and luck."

"Well, I think we need all those things to cross that rickety bridge," said Christina.

Mimi gave Christina a comforting hug. "Papa and I will go first," she said. "Just don't look down!"

They were halfway across before Christina gingerly placed her foot on the bridge. Grant and the others followed her with Pemba and Socks bringing up the rear.

"This is fun!" Grant said, jumping up and down to make the bridge sway even more than it already was.

Despite what Mimi had told her, Christina glanced down. Between the planks, she could see the frigid water far, far, below and the huge gray rocks that made it splash angrily. She imagined how cold it would feel to fall in!

"Just put one foot in front of the other," Uncle Mike encouraged her.

Christina was nearly halfway across when she noticed a prayer flag waving wildly above her head. It was a different shape and color than all the others and the writing was not faded. She reached up and tugged on the green flag that easily came loose. She was about to look at it when she heard Socks' hooves hit the wooden bridge:

CLICKETY CLACK!

HE WAS CHARGING RIGHT AT HER!

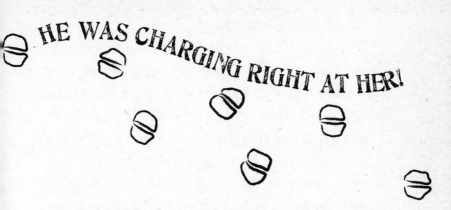

Christina clutched the rail with all her might while the bridge bucked and bounced under the frightened yak's weight. The swirling, frigid water and jagged rocks zoomed toward her and she could feel herself slipping down...

"Christina! Christina!" Uncle Mike said, gently tapping her cheek with his gloved hand. "Everything's okay!"

Christina slowly opened her eyes. She could see Mimi and Papa holding Socks' rope on the other side of the ravine. Grant, Dawa, and Lhakpa were standing over her with worried looks. The air was cold, but her cheeks burned.

"Did I faint?" she asked.

"Nothing to be embarrassed about," Uncle Mike said. "The thin air mixed with a frightened, charging yak is enough to make anyone faint! Now let's get off this bridge."

Christina and the other kids found a rock, flat as a giant turtle's back, and lay down. The sun peeked through the gray clouds. Christina wished she could **bask** in its warmth all day! But Everest, looking larger and larger on the horizon, was almost daring her now. Uncle Mike and Dave had to reach the summit so Mimi could write her book, even if someone or something was trying to stop them!

Christina rolled onto her side and felt something in her pocket. In all the fear and excitement on the bridge, she had forgotten about the flag!

"Where did you get that?" Dawa asked.

"It was flapping over the bridge," Christina explained. "It looks brand new."

"I don't think it's good luck to tear down a prayer flag," Lhakpa said.

Dawa read the flag aloud:

"This is your last chance to turn back, or you will become a piece of ice on Chomolungma!"

The Breathtaking Mystery on Mount Everest

12

DANGER BY THE FOOT

"Are we there yet?" Grant whined, lifting his knees high in snow that was getting deeper. "After six days, I feel like a walking robot."

"Look on the bright side," Christina said. "At least you haven't had to take a bath in six days!"

"True," said Grant. "But I'm worried that Papa's beard may reach his waist. Just look at it."

Christina smiled at Papa. He did not look like the same person. Normally clean shaven, his face was salt and peppery with a stubbly beard. Uncle Mike and Dave had beards too. She had seen pictures of Everest climbers with ice hanging from their beards and wondered if that's what would happen to them.

Christina rubbed her cold cheeks with her thick gloves and looked around. She saw nothing but snow and gray rocks. She felt like she was inside Mimi's freezer. The last time Uncle Mike had checked his thermometer it was 20 degrees. "I wish I could grow a beard," she said. "At least it would help keep my face warm."

Finally Christina could see orange and green and blue polka dots in the snow. They were tents!

Uncle Mike yelled and jumped for joy. "That's Base Camp, isn't it, Pemba?"

"Yes, my friend," Pemba answered. "You have made it!"

"Whose tents are those?" Grant asked. "Are there other people here?"

"I guess we're not the only expedition," Uncle Mike answered.

"Let's get across this glacier and down on the moraine," Uncle Mike said.

"Glacier?" Christina asked.

"You're on the edge of the famous Khumbu Glacier right now," he said.

"Now, wait a minute," Grant said.

Christina knew that was a signal that about a million questions were about to follow.

"Are you talking about that stuff on top of Mimi's lemon pie?" Grant asked.

Everyone exchanged confused looks, but fortunately, Mimi understood what he was talking about and explained. "No, Grant," she said. "The stuff on my lemon pie is *meringue*; it's made out of egg whites. A *moraine* is the boulders, stones and other stuff brought here by the glacier."

"Well, I really don't know what a glacier is either," said Grant, frustrated.

"A glacier is really thick ice made of layers and layers of snow," said Mimi. "The cool thing is, pardon the pun, that snow in the glacier probably fell thousands of years ago. Once it gets really, really thick, it begins to move. Usually it moves slowly, maybe an inch or two a day, but sometimes it can move 100 feet in a day!"

"Don't worry," Uncle Mike said, "I've read that the Khumbu Glacier moves about three feet a day. We can run faster than that."

"We better put on our snow glasses," Dave reminded. "The last thing we need is for someone to look at snow until it hurts their eyes, or go snow blind."

Christina also had a million questions, but she found it hard to make long sentences. She had never been at this altitude before, at least not outside of an airplane.

"Why," Christina asked, breathless, "Is... the...ice...blue?"

"It has to do with the light rays," Dave explained. "You know that light is made up of different colors, right?"

Danger by the Foot

"Yes, I know ROY G BIV," Grant said, proud that he finally knew something. "Red, Orange, Yellow, Green, Blue, Indigo and Violet."

"Wow," Dave said. "That's right. Well, the red and yellow don't have as much energy and get absorbed by the ice and snow in the glacier. But the blue has more energy and it gets scattered around and that's what we see."

"Th-Th-That's...not...all...I...see," Christina said, between deep breaths. "I...see...a...boot. And...I...think...there's...still...a...foot...in...it!"

BECAUSE IT'S THERE!

"Unfortunately, it's not unusual to find dead bodies and parts of dead bodies on Everest," Uncle Mike explained. "This is a very dangerous place. I want you to be very careful."

Pemba nodded with a serious look on his face. "More than 175 climbers have died trying to climb Mount Everest," he said. "About 60 of those have been sherpas like me."

"That's awful!" Grant exclaimed. "Why don't they bring them off the mountain or at least bury them here?"

"Many of the bodies are in places that are impossible to reach," Pemba explained. "And it's too difficult for climbers to carry the weight of a body off the mountain. They might die themselves if they tried."

No sooner had Pemba finished speaking than Mimi, who was walking ahead of Christina, suddenly got much shorter. All Christina could see was her head above the snow.

"Help!" Mimi yelped.

Pemba and Papa saw what had happened and pulled Mimi's arms until she plopped on top of the snow like a seal.

"What happened?" Mimi asked, grimacing and reaching for her ankle.

"I think you found a crevasse, or crack in the ice that had been covered by a thin layer of snow!" Pemba exclaimed.

"You OK, Mimi?" Christina asked, staring at her grandmother's twisted foot.

"I will be," she said with a pained smile. "But I think this is the end of the journey for me. I'm pretty sure my ankle is broken!"

Uncle Mike was already on the satellite phone calling for help. "They'll have a helicopter here in an hour," he said.

Papa looked worried, but tried to lighten the mood. "I guess that means no more 'ice screams' for Mimi!" he remarked.

Christina thought about the warnings she had received on the journey. Now, Mimi was hurt! *Sure, writing a great book was important, but was it time to turn back before something worse happened?* She looked into Uncle Mike's glacier-blue eyes and asked, "Why do you....really want to...climb Everest?"

"My reason's the same as George Mallory's," answered Uncle Mike. "He was a British mountaineer in the 1920s and when a reporter asked him that question he answered, 'Because it's there!'"

By the time they crossed the glacier and reached Base Camp a helicopter was stirring up a blizzard of snow. Christina's heart dropped when she saw it was only large enough to carry Mimi and Papa back to Kathmandu.

"Take care of each other!" Mimi yelled with a wave as she was loaded into the helicopter.

"Remember, we're only a phone call away!" Papa said, waving the satellite phone and blowing them a kiss.

The thought of staying at Base Camp without Mimi and Papa was a little frightening to Christina. But Pemba had explained that a sherpa named Mingmar would take good care of them after he, Uncle Mike, and Dave left. Christina was also thankful that Dawa and Lhakpa were with them. She rested and breathed in oxygen from one of Uncle Mike's tanks while the others cleared stones for their camp site and unpacked the tents.

"That glacier sure did make a mess," Grant said.

Christina looked slowly around the base camp. It felt like being in a bowl. Himalayan peaks surrounded it like dinosaurs. The ridges reminded her of a stegosaurus' back. But surprisingly, Everest was not visible from the Base Camp.

Grant's frantic screams interrupted Christina's thoughts. She was not surprised to see her brother wrapped like a cocoon in a tangle of ropes. Dawa and Lhakpa, both laughing, worked to set him free.

"Your brother is a bit clumsy!" Lhakpa yelled. "I don't think he is ready to be a sherpa!"

Christina laughed too, until she noticed a man standing in the door of a large tent farther up the campsite. She hoped he was not Mingmar, the sherpa Pemba had told them about. Her eyes might be playing tricks on her, but he looked like he was wearing a green cap!

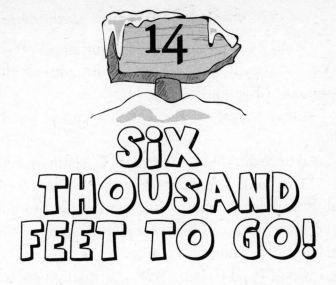

SiX THOUSAND FEET TO GO!

Socks pawed at the ground impatiently as if to say, "Don't forget about me! I've still got all this heavy stuff on my back!"

Uncle Mike and Dave unloaded the rest of their oxygen tanks and stacked the red, green, and yellow cylinders like firewood. Without them the climb would be impossible. Christina was having trouble breathing at this altitude, but the men still had more than 6,000 feet to climb to the summit!

"Those look like missiles," Grant remarked.

"Well, they're sort of like missiles," Dave said. "They'll help us shoot straight to the summit of Everest!"

Pemba surprised them with a cup of piping hot tea.

"Where'd... this come from?" Christina asked.

"The guide companies have a cook tent here all the time," he said. "It has a machine to boil and purify water. I just scooped up some of the glacier snow and put it inside."

"Cool!" said Grant. "We're drinking new tea made from old snow!"

Christina was grateful for the tea. She enjoyed its warmth sliding down her throat and its familiar smell in her freezing nostrils. She removed her gloves and felt the wonderful warmth on her hands.

Pemba also gave each of them a special plastic bottle.

"What's this for?" Grant asked.

"There is a bathroom tent near the cook tent," Pemba said. "But during the middle of the night, it is a very cold place." He tapped the

84

bottle. "That's when this becomes your bathroom!"

When they were finished with their tea, Uncle Mike and Dave set up the global positioning system, which most people called GPS. They would carry a device to allow Christina and the others to watch their progress up the mountain and help them be found if they got lost. They had just finished when the squawking satellite phone made them all jump.

This is Papa, everyone OK up there?

Yes, we're fine! Uncle Mike answered. *How's Mom?*

She's resting comfortably. She just has a huge cast on her foot. Anyone want to guess what color it is?

RED! Her favorite color! they all shouted with relief.

Right! Everyone sleep tight! I'll buzz you tomorrow! Over and out!

After another supper of potato soup, they watched the sun's last golden rays sinking behind the majestic mountains.

"Rest well!" Pemba said, slapping Uncle Mike and Dave on the back. "Tomorrow we climb Everest!"

When Christina and Dawa headed for their tent, Christina decided they should pay a visit to the bathroom tent first. There were creepy shadows on the ground, but she did not want to use the bathroom in a bottle!

"Look!" Dawa said, pointing to the same tent where Christina had seen the suspicious man earlier.

Christina's eyes had not played tricks on her. Inside was the green cap man from the store in Namche Bazaar!

NO O?

After a long, cold, and restless night, Christina awoke to the sound of angry voices outside their tent.

She stretched and worked her way out of the mummy-shaped sleeping bag.

Uncle Mike was pacing frantically with his hands on his hips, staring at the fresh snow on the ground. "Who would do this?" he asked.

"Do what?" Christina asked.

"Our oxygen tanks are gone!" Dave exclaimed.

Where the pile of tanks was stacked the day before, there was nothing but a pile of stacked stones and triangle prints in the snow!

"We're just going to have to try and make it without oxygen!" Uncle Mike said determinedly. "We've all come too far to give up now! Reinhold

Messner and Peter Habeler were the first to climb Everest without oxygen and there've been several since then. We can do it too!"

Christina was alarmed to hear her uncle talk this way, but knew him well enough to know he would try it. She thought of the boot with the foot inside and looked at her uncle. *We've got to find those oxygen tanks,* she thought.

Soon the others were awake. They walked underneath a shrine of prayer flags fluttering in the wind. Ice axes were stacked underneath waiting to be blessed. Lhakpa said it was a Base Camp tradition.

Christina looked up to see two ravens circling overhead. Dawa saw them too. "That's a bad omen," she said.

"Let's take...another look...at those stacked stones," Christina said, still short of breath. "We have to...find out who...wants to keep us off Everest!"

One by one they dismantled the stacked stones. Near the bottom, Christina saw the jagged corner of a black piece of paper! She tugged until it came free and handed it to Dawa to translate.

When Dawa finished, Christina regretted that she hadn't told the adults about the first note sooner. Maybe they would've known what to do. It was too late now and Uncle Mike and Dave were in great danger!

The note said:

You didn't turn back,
but we will win.
Dead men don't
need oxygen!

16

COLD SARDINES

"Uncle Mike, you can't go...without oxygen!" Christina cried.

"Don't worry," Pemba said. "We will be fine without oxygen for a while. I've called a porter. That's someone who carries supplies on his back. He'll bring oxygen to Camp One after we clear the Khumbu Icefall."

"What's the Khumbu Icefall?" Grant asked.

"It's a part of the glacier that broke off down a steep slope," Uncle Mike explained patiently.

"I wish we could go too!" Lhakpa said.

"Someday you will," Pemba said. "But now you must help take care of Base Camp."

"Yes," Uncle Mike agreed. "Do not leave this camp, and let the support staff member Mingmar know if you need help. Most importantly, stay close to the satellite phone! But don't call us too often. We'll need all our air for climbing and don't need to waste it on talking!"

The three men strapped the crampons on their boots, swung what looked like miles of red and blue rope across their shoulders, tucked ice axes in their climbing harnesses, and finally swung heavy packs onto their backs. They clanked all over when the kids hugged them goodbye!

Uncle Mike, Dave, and Pemba wobbled toward the icefall like astronauts walking on the moon. Christina could see other climbers far ahead. They were nothing but tiny specks against the snow. "Grant, can...I borrow...your binoculars?" she asked.

"Sure," he said, trotting off to the tent for them.

Christina focused on the group ahead of Uncle Mike's team. She was shocked to see that

Cold Sardines

the entire group wore bright green ski caps! *Were they the same people who stole the oxygen?*

"You should get inside and rest, Tia," Grant told her. "You look pale."

Christina climbed back into her sleeping bag and strapped on her oxygen mask. Uncle Mike made her keep the only one that hadn't been stolen, but she wished he had it with him. She watched the slow-moving blips on the GPS screen that showed her climbing team and tried hard not to worry.

Christina, Christina, are you there? the phone squawked.

Uncle Mike? she answered. In the background she heard the crunch of snow under boots and the clank of ice axes biting into ice.

We're almost over the icefall! A porter will be here tomorrow with the oxygen, so don't worry! Over and out!

The kids spent the day playing card games, snacking on granola bars, and watching the blips. When night came, they packed into one tent like sardines in a can. It was cramped and cold, but warmer than outside where Socks was standing. Christina felt sorry for him, but there was certainly no room for a yak in the tent. She could hear his bell tinkle softly from time to time. Dawa assured her he had plenty of fur to keep him warm.

"Grant," Christina whispered. "You scared?"

"Let's see, we're four kids high in the mountains with our relatives hours away," he said. "I would have to say I'm a little scared."

Pemba had warned them they would hear creaking and cracking of the glacier ice, but it was the distant high-pitched yelps in the distance that bothered Christina. She remembered what the lama had told them. *Could it be the sounds of a yeti?*

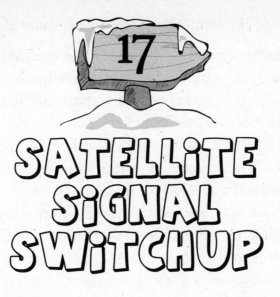

SATELLITE SIGNAL SWITCHUP

Christina tossed and turned. The winds howled louder and louder, drowning out every sound but the constant jingling of Socks' bell. The tent rattled and rippled and she feared it might blow away with them inside. Christina stared at the phone. She wanted to call Uncle Mike or Mimi or someone on the Base Camp support staff, but what would they be able to do?

The winds had finally quieted down when Grant asked, "Is it morning yet?"

"The clock says it is, but it's still kind of dark," said Christina.

Dawa yawned. "I think I know what the problem is," she said. She carefully unzipped the tent and buckets of snow that had blocked the light of day fell inside!

"That was some snowstorm last night!" Lhakpa said, tunneling out of the tent, which now looked more like an igloo.

The frosty air took Christina's breath away and burned the inside of her nose. She was relieved to see that Socks had survived the storm although icicles were hanging from his fur and horns. He snorted nervously.

Binoculars in hand, she scanned the horizon, worried about what Uncle Mike, Dave, and Pemba had gone through during the snowstorm. There was nothing to see but white and gray striped mountainsides and plumes of snow blowing off their peaks like smoke from a chimney. Then, the phone squawked. Maybe it was them!

Christina dove back into the tent. She heard voices, but they didn't belong to their team! Her satellite phone was picking up someone else's static-filled conversation!

We're far ahead of them, a deep voice said. *Without oxygen, they'll never beat us...*

A woman's voice replied,...*never find that oxygen...too afraid...my book...first...*

When the phone turned to nothing but static, Christina pushed the button to reach Uncle Mike. No answer. And the GPS monitor screen was black.

"I'm worried...about our team," Christina confessed to the others who had joined her in the tent. "I doubt that porter can get here...with more oxygen...after this snowstorm. We've got to...figure out...where the stolen oxygen is...and why someone is...trying to beat us to the summit!"

"What about our last clue?" Grant said. "Dead men don't need oxygen—what were they talking about?"

"Our team will die without oxygen," Dawa said.

Christina was thinking. "What if it...has two meanings," she said between gasps. "Pemba said there are frozen bodies...all over this mountain. What if the oxygen...is hidden near one of them?"

"Yeah!" exclaimed Grant. "That woman's voice on the phone said we'd be too afraid. That's something we'd be afraid of!"

"All that oxygen is heavy," Lhakpa added. "One person couldn't have taken it very far."

"Let's go on our own expedition!" Grant suggested with **dauntless** determination. "We know there's a body on the glacier. We saw the foot!"

Normally, Christina would be all for such an idea. But today, she knew her altitude sickness, which seemed to be getting worse instead of better, would not allow her to go. Grant was thinking the same thing.

"Lhakpa and I could go, and you and Dawa could wait here by the phone," he said. "Socks can come with us to carry the oxygen tanks!"

Despite fear for their safety, Christina gave Grant their extra phone and helped them into their snowsuits. She gave Grant a bear hug. "Please...be careful!" she warned.

"Don't worry, Sis!" Grant said confidently. "I've got a sherpa with me, remember?"

Lhakpa grinned proudly.

Christina and Dawa watched Grant and Lhakpa until they disappeared behind a snow drift. When they turned to go back into the tent, she saw something much more frightening than a dead body. Dawa saw it too and turned white as the snow. It was a giant footprint!

AVALANCHE!

Christina knew this adventure would be hard. But with a grandmother in the hospital, an uncle on the most dangerous mountain in the world, a little brother searching for a dead body, and a man-eating yeti on the loose, could it get any worse?

Christina reviewed the mound of mysteries in her mind. She was still puzzled why someone would want to keep them from reaching the summit. First, it was Uncle Mike's life-long goal. Who would have a problem with that? Second, he wanted Mimi to write a book about the experience so children would know what it was like. Maybe they might want to climb Everest some day!

Wait a minute, Christina thought. During the phone conversation she overheard, the woman had said something about a book...

She pushed the buttons to reach Mimi and Papa's phone. *Christina, is that you?* Mimi asked. *I've been trying to reach you. Heard there was a big snowstorm last night. Are you OK?*

Christina didn't want Mimi to worry. *We're OK, Mimi,* she said. *How's your ankle?*

Mimi answered, *A little itchy inside the cast, but Papa's taking good care of me! And guess what? I've already started the book. By the time Uncle Mike reaches the summit, all I'll have to do is add the happy ending!*

Christina hoped there would be a happy ending to add! *Mimi,* she asked, *did anyone know that you were planning to write this book?*

I mentioned it to some other writers at a publisher's convention, Mimi answered.

BEEP. BEEP. Grant was trying to call.

Sorry, Mimi, I have to go, Christina said, pushing the buttons to answer Grant.

Christina! Grant exclaimed. *We can see a black glove sticking out of the snow...I think there's*

Avalanche!

a body attached! Something's buried in a mound of snow...

Christina heard a deafening roar.

Dawa darted to the tent door.
"AVALANCHE!" she yelled.

YETI IN HIGH HEELS

A river of snow flowed down the mountain throwing sparkling crystals in the air, thick as steam. *Were Grant and Lhakpa trapped underneath?* Christina fretted. She grabbed the phone and frantically punched numbers.

GRANT! GRANT! COME IN GRANT! she yelled. Static crackled. *GRANT, PLEASE ANSWER!!!*

Christina gasped for air, felt like she might faint again, when a voice punched through the static.

WE'RE OK! Grant hollered. *And we found the oxygen!*

But how'd you get out? Christina asked.

We were holding Socks' rope! Grant exclaimed. *He pulled us out like a bulldozer! I'm calling Uncle Mike now to see if Pemba can come back down and meet us to get the oxygen.*

Roger! Christina replied. *I can't get them on my phone. Maybe you can. Keep me informed!*

Dawa was as relieved as Christina that the avalanche hadn't harmed their brothers. "Don't worry," she told Christina. "My father has been up and down the mountain many times. He is very strong. He will get the oxygen!"

Hours later, Grant finally called Christina to tell her Pemba had the oxygen and was getting it to Uncle Mike and Dave. Now, they had a good chance to make it to the summit! He and Lhakpa were headed back to Base Camp.

"What was that?" Dawa asked, fearful the yeti might be nearby.

Christina laughed. "It's just my stomach growling," she said. Christina hadn't felt hungry since they made it to Base Camp, but now she really wanted something to eat. She was surprised that no one from the Base Camp support staff had checked on them. "Let's go down to the kitchen tent and see if we can figure out how to make tea and heat some canned soup."

The sun was once again sinking behind the mountains and their flashlight beams danced on the snow. Empty tents lined the paths waiting patiently for their adventurous owners to return.

CRUNCH! CRUNCH! CRUNCH!

Christina and Dawa heard the crunch of footsteps following them. They stopped and looked. The footsteps stopped. When they started walking again, the footsteps started up again.

"Let's turn...with our flashlights...on three," Christina whispered, not knowing who or what she would see behind them, human or beast. She hoped it was only Mingmar, the Base Camp support staff member. "One, two, three!"

A stocky man shielded his eyes from the lights. He was wearing a green cap! "RUN!" Christina yelled.

Christina and Dawa cut between two tents. A loud "GRRRR!" stopped them in their tracks. This time it wasn't Christina's stomach. It was a big, hairy, yeti!

The choices weren't good. Turn back and run into the man in the green cap or face this vicious beast that had raised its furry paws at them! There was no time to decide. The girls ran back through the tents and dove inside one that was unzipped. Shivering, they cowered in a dark corner and listened to the crunch of giant feet in the snow outside. Suddenly, they heard more sounds. There were muffled noises coming from the opposite corner of the tent. Someone was inside the tent with them!

Christina knew she couldn't turn on the flashlight or their hiding place would be spoiled. She swallowed hard and slithered across the tent floor, feeling her way until she touched an arm! The muffled sounds started again. Christina reached up and felt a face with tape where the

The Breathtaking Mystery on Mount Everest

mouth should have been. She decided to take a chance that he was a good guy and ripped off the tape. The man gasped.

"Who are you?" Christina whispered.

"Base Camp support staff—Mingmar!" he answered, gasping for air. "A man in a green cap forced me in here and tied me up. He said I would get in the way."

"So that's why you haven't checked on us!" Christina exclaimed, working frantically to untie the rope around his wrists.

Dawa had just crawled over to help when the yeti roared outside. A paw with razor sharp claws ripped through the tent canvas right above their heads!

Mingmar yanked his arms free of the loosened ropes and jumped to his feet. "Let's get out of here!" he cried.

As the yeti stumbled along behind them, Christina flashed her light back and saw the man in the green cap chasing them as well. She flipped off the light as she and Darma once again dove into an open tent. Christina could feel a table inside covered with papers. She also felt a ski cap and had an idea. She placed the cap over the flashlight to cut the amount of light. When she turned it on, she could see that the ski cap was green, just like the team she had seen going up the mountain. What luck! Now they were in the tent where she saw the green cap man on the day they arrived!

She looked at the papers on the table and saw chapter headings and an outline about Mount Everest.

"I'm going to notify the authorities!" Mingmar said, tiptoeing out the tent's back door.

He'd only been gone a few minutes when Christina's forgotten phone squawked loudly. She grabbed it to turn it down, hoping the yeti and Green Cap hadn't heard. It was Grant.

We're at the tent, he said. *Where are you?*

The yeti is after us, whispered Christina. She didn't have time to say more. The yeti had heard the phone and was standing in the doorway! Christina yanked the ski cap off the flashlight and shined it in the monster's face. She grabbed

Dawa's arm and dashed toward the tent's back door. But Green Cap had already thought of that. He was standing there!

Arms raised, the yeti moved toward them, growling. This time there was no place to run. A sharp yell split the night air and startled the yeti. Before Christina knew what was happening, the yeti fell to the ground and she saw Grant and Lhakpa sitting on its back!

Christina whirled in time to see Mingmar tackle Green Cap. "Don't worry," he said. "The authorities will be here soon."

"Whew!" Christina said, wiping her forehead. "I didn't think we'd get out of this one!"

"I could have used my karate skills," Grant bragged, "but I didn't need to. I thought it would be harder to tackle a yeti!"

"I don't think you tackled a yeti," Christina said.

"I did too!" Grant cried. "What do you mean?"

"You know how an animal's eyes usually glow when you shine a light into them?" asked Christina.

"Yeah," Grant replied.

"This yeti's eyes didn't glow," she said. "In fact, I never saw it blink!"

A puzzle was quickly coming together in Christina's mind. She thought about the papers in the tent and she remembered that Mimi had shared her Everest book idea at a publisher's convention.

"I think this yeti...is a writer!" she exclaimed.

"What?!" Grant, Lhakpa, and Dawa yelled in unison.

Christina yanked the beast's shaggy head and it came off in her hand! Everyone gasped. The yeti was an attractive woman with long brown hair! She looked at them sheepishly.

"You wanted...to beat our team to Everest...and be the first to write a children's mystery about it!" Christina shouted. "If your team got there first, you could claim that Mimi stole your idea!"

Christina shined her flashlight on Green Cap. It was her first good look at him. "You're a sherpa!" she exclaimed. "You wrote the notes, didn't you?"

"I was only doing what I was hired to do," he confessed. "I mailed many of the notes to her. I didn't know what she did with them."

"She delivered one to my grandmother's house, in high heels, no doubt," Christina said, remembering the triangle-shaped footprints in the wet grass.

"I guess she thought the note would frighten us enough to stay away," Grant said. "She doesn't know us very well!"

Christina agreed. "Even stolen oxygen and the yells of a yeti didn't scare us away! Our team is going to beat hers to the top and Mimi's going to finish her book while these characters are sitting in jail!"

TOP OF
THE WORLD

Days later, the kids huddled anxiously around the GPS monitor. The weather had cleared and the equipment was working as it should. The three bleeps, which were really Uncle Mike, Dave, and Pemba, were getting close to the summit. During the past six days, they had clawed their way up the mountain. If they were going to make it, today would be the day!

Squawk...*Christina, can you hear me?* Mimi asked through the phone. She was waiting at a Kathmandu hotel while Papa had returned to Base Camp to be with the kids.

Yes, Mimi, Christina answered. *And I can finally talk without gasping. I'm acclimated!*

Great! Mimi said. *Let me know as soon as they get there. I only have one more chapter to write!*

Mimi, Christina said. *Did you include something about protecting the mountains and taking back everything you bring?*

Yes, said Mimi. *A whole chapter!*

And did you tell about our hero yak, Socks? Grant asked.

Of course, Mimi said with a laugh. *And our friends Pemba, Dawa, and Lhakpa!*

Hold on, Mimi, Christina said. *Uncle Mike is calling!*

Uncle Mike? Christina said.

Almost there, guys! Uncle Mike huffed between puffs of oxygen. *Thanks for all your help. Couldn't have done it without you!*

Christina could hear the wind howling by the phone. She could almost feel the cold in Uncle Mike's voice.

Is your beard frozen? Grant asked.

Yes, it is, Grant, Uncle Mike answered. *And you'd love this. We all have icicle b-b-boogers!*

Grant pumped his fist in the air. "Yessss!" he cried.

Did you beat the green team? Christina asked.

We left them behind hours ago, Uncle Mike said. *Hold on, I want you to hear this...*

The kids heard crunching footsteps, shuffling, the ting of ice picks and finally,

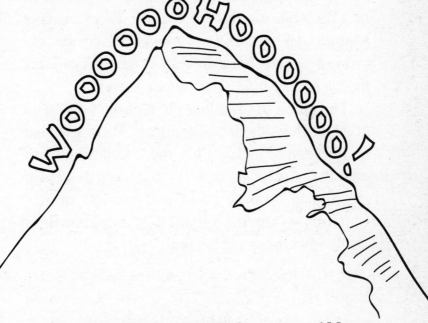

We are standing at 29,028 feet on top of Mount Everest! Uncle Mike shouted. *Everest is holding us up high enough to touch the sky! We are dancing a victory dance for all of you!*

The kids exchanged excited high-fives.

What do you see? Grant asked.

Uncle Mike's voice sounded a bit choked up. *It's the most beautiful sight I've ever seen! I'm standing at the top of the globe and I feel like the world is turning beneath me. I'm looking down on the clouds like an angel in heaven! There are other mountaintops peeking up through the clouds, but we're above them all. Now I know why they call this the top of the world. You can see forever!*

Papa took the satellite phone from Grant and grabbed the kids in a group hug. *We're so proud of you, son,* he said, his voice cracking with emotion. *Come back safe! We can't wait to see you!*

"And tell you all about our own adventure," Christina whispered to Grant. "You know how Uncle Mike likes excitement!"

THE END

About the Author

Carole Marsh is an author and publisher who has written many works of fiction and non-fiction for young readers. She travels throughout the United States and around the world to research her books. In 1979 Carole Marsh was named Communicator of the Year for her corporate communications work with major national and international corporations.

Marsh is the founder and CEO of Gallopade International, established in 1979. Today, Gallopade International is widely recognized as a leading source of educational materials for every state and many countries. Marsh and Gallopade were recipients of the 2004 Teachers' Choice Award. Marsh has written more than 50 Carole Marsh Mysteries™. In 2007, she was named Georgia Author of the Year. Years ago, her children, Michele and Michael, were the original characters in her mystery books. Today, they continue the Carole Marsh Books tradition by working at Gallopade. By adding grandchildren Grant and Christina as new mystery characters, she has continued the tradition for a third generation.

Ms. Marsh welcomes correspondence from her readers. You can e-mail her at fanclub@gallopade.com, visit carolemarshmysteries.com, or write to her in care of Gallopade International, P.O. Box 2779, Peachtree City, Georgia, 30269 USA.

Built-In Book Club

Talk About It!

1. Have you ever climbed a mountain? Would you be brave enough to climb Mount Everest?

2. Since so many people have died trying to climb Mount Everest, why do you think people want to do it?

3. Do you believe the yeti is a myth or a real animal? How would you prove it?

4. If you were planning an expedition to Mount Everest what is the one thing you couldn't do without?

5. If you found a mysterious note before taking a dangerous trip, would you tell an adult?

6. Would you like to have a yak for a pet?

7. What should be done about the problem of hikers leaving trash on Himalayan trails and Mount Everest?

8. Do you think tourists have helped or hurt the Sherpas?

9. What was your favorite part of the story?

10. What would have been the result if the other person had published a book about climbing Everest before Mimi published her book?

Built-In Book Club

Bring it to Life!

1. Write a funny story about a yeti. Be sure to include a description of his home and what he eats for dinner!

2. Try some Sherpa tea (without the salt and yak butter)! Have an adult help you boil six cups of water. Steep three tea bags in the hot water for three to four minutes. Add 1/3 cup of sugar and 1/3 cup non-dairy creamer.

3. Pretend you've just met the yak that will carry your equipment to Base Camp. Make up a name for him and draw his picture!

4. Find a good photo of Mount Everest. Working quickly, use spoons and other utensils to mold a bowl of ice cream into its shape. Eat your way to the top!

5. Make a glacier! Find rocks, sand and twigs and place them in a quart-size sealable plastic bag. Fill with water and freeze. Later, place your glacier in the sun and watch as it melts and creates a moraine.

6. There is always snow on Mount Everest and no two snowflakes are exactly alike. Design your own snowflake, and then hang it in your window to remind you of your adventure with Christina and Grant!

7. Make a prayer flag! Cut a colorful piece of cloth into a square. Write something special on it. Then, hang it outside to flutter in the wind.

Mount Everest
Trivia

1. Many mountaineers have a goal of climbing the Seven Summits. These are the highest mountains on each continent!

2. Edmund Hillary and Tenzing Norgay made it to the summit of Mount Everest on May 29, 1953.

3. Edmund Hillary was a beekeeper in New Zealand before he became a famous mountaineer!

4. When climbers reach 26,000 feet on Mount Everest, they have reached the area known as the Death Zone.

5. Junko Tabei of Japan became the first woman to reach the summit of Mount Everest in 1975.

6. The first American to reach the summit of Mount Everest was James Whittaker in 1963.

7. About 120 corpses or dead bodies are on Mount Everest.

8. The body of George Mallory, who tried to reach the Everest summit in 1924, was found in 1999.

9. Some people believe that George Mallory and his climbing partner, Andrew Irvine, were the first people to reach the summit. Scientists would love to find the camera Irvine carried, develop the film and find out for sure!

10. The youngest person to reach the Mount Everest summit was 15-year-old Temba Tsheri Sherpa of Nepal in 2001.

Glossary

abode: the place where one stays or lives

SAD **abominable:** very hateful

acclimate: become accustomed to a new environment

SAD **altitude:** vertical distance or elevation above any point or base-level, such as the sea

avalanche: a large mass of snow and ice sliding down a mountain

SAD **bask:** to warm the body in the sunlight

SAD **crag:** a rugged, rocky projection on a cliff or ledge

Glossary

dauntless: fearless

expedition: a journey or trip for a particular purpose

omen: a sign supposed to forecast the future

Scavenger Hunt

Want to have some fun? Let's go on a scavenger hunt! See if you can find the items below related to the mystery. (*Teachers: You have permission to reproduce this page for your students.*)

1. ___ a cup of hot chocolate

2. ___ a hiking boot

3. ___ a compass

4. ___ a toy walkie-talkie

5. ___ a picture of a yak

6. ___ a ski cap

7. ___ a flashlight

8. ___ a glove

9. ___ a high-heeled shoe

10. ___ a can of soup

Visit the <u>carolemarshmysteries.com</u> website to:

- Join the Carole Marsh Mysteries™ Fan Club!

- Write a letter to Christina, Grant, Mimi, or Papa!

- Cast your vote for where the next mystery should take place!

- Find fascinating facts about the countries where the mysteries take place!

- Track your reading on an international map!

- Take the Fact or Fiction online quiz!

- Find out where the *Mystery Girl* is flying next!